BBC
Bob the Builder™
Bob's Boots
D0470270

One morning Bob walked into his front room carrying a big box.

"Look, Finn!" he said excitedly. "The postman has just delivered this. I wonder what's inside?"

Finn pressed his nose up against his glass tank and watched Bob open the box.

"My new boots have arrived!" cried Bob, holding them up for Finn to see. "What do you think of them?" he asked.

The goldfish did a back-flip. **Splash!**

He really liked Bob's new boots!

"I think I'll wear my new boots to work," said Bob.

When he walked out into the yard, Wendy was giving the machines their jobs for the day.

"Lofty, you're with Bob today," she said. "Muck and Scoop, you're with me."

"Morning, Wendy," called Bob.

"Morning, Bob," Wendy replied.

Bob walked around the yard proudly.

"What do you think of my new boots?" he asked them.

"They're very smart," replied Wendy.

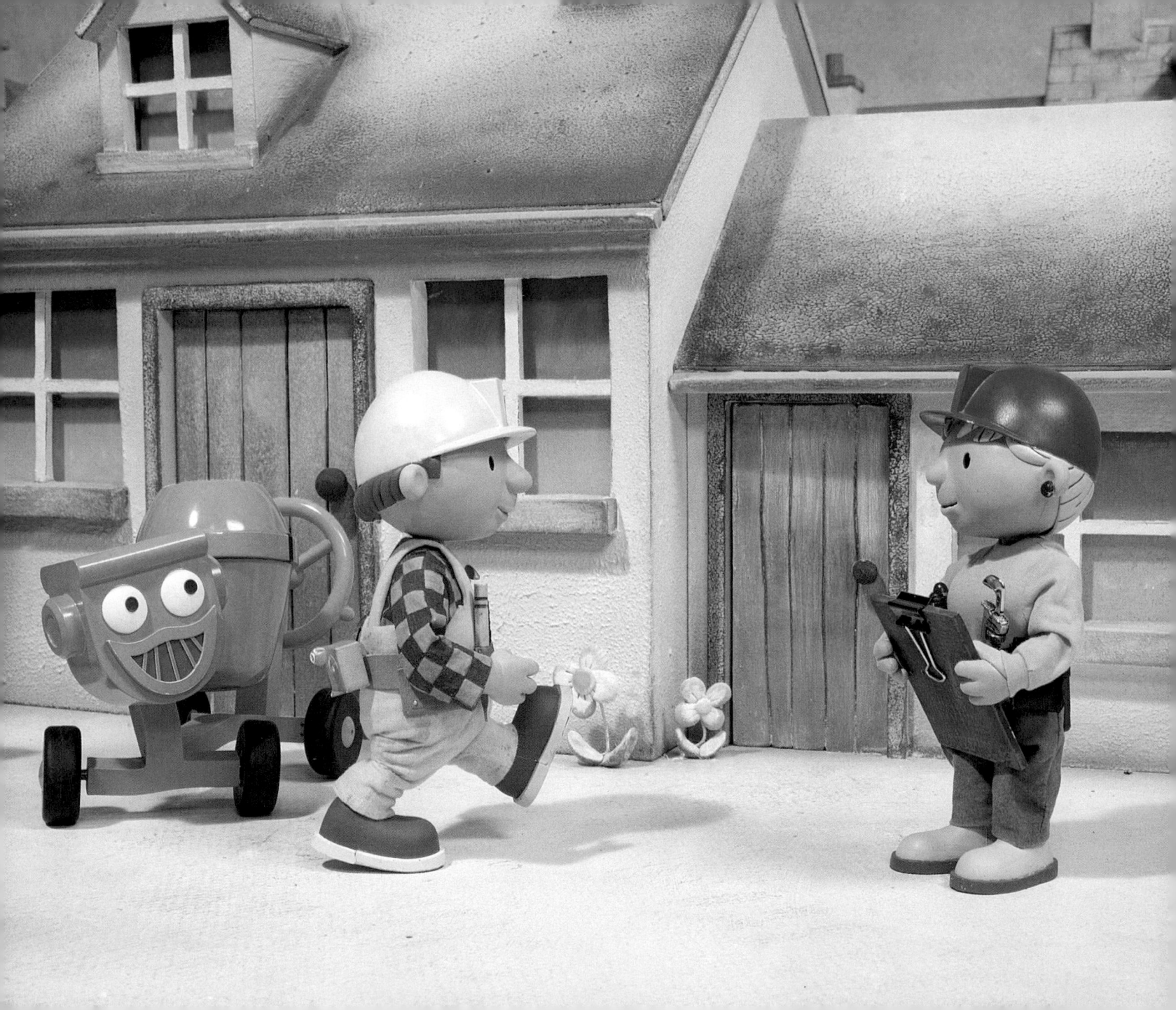

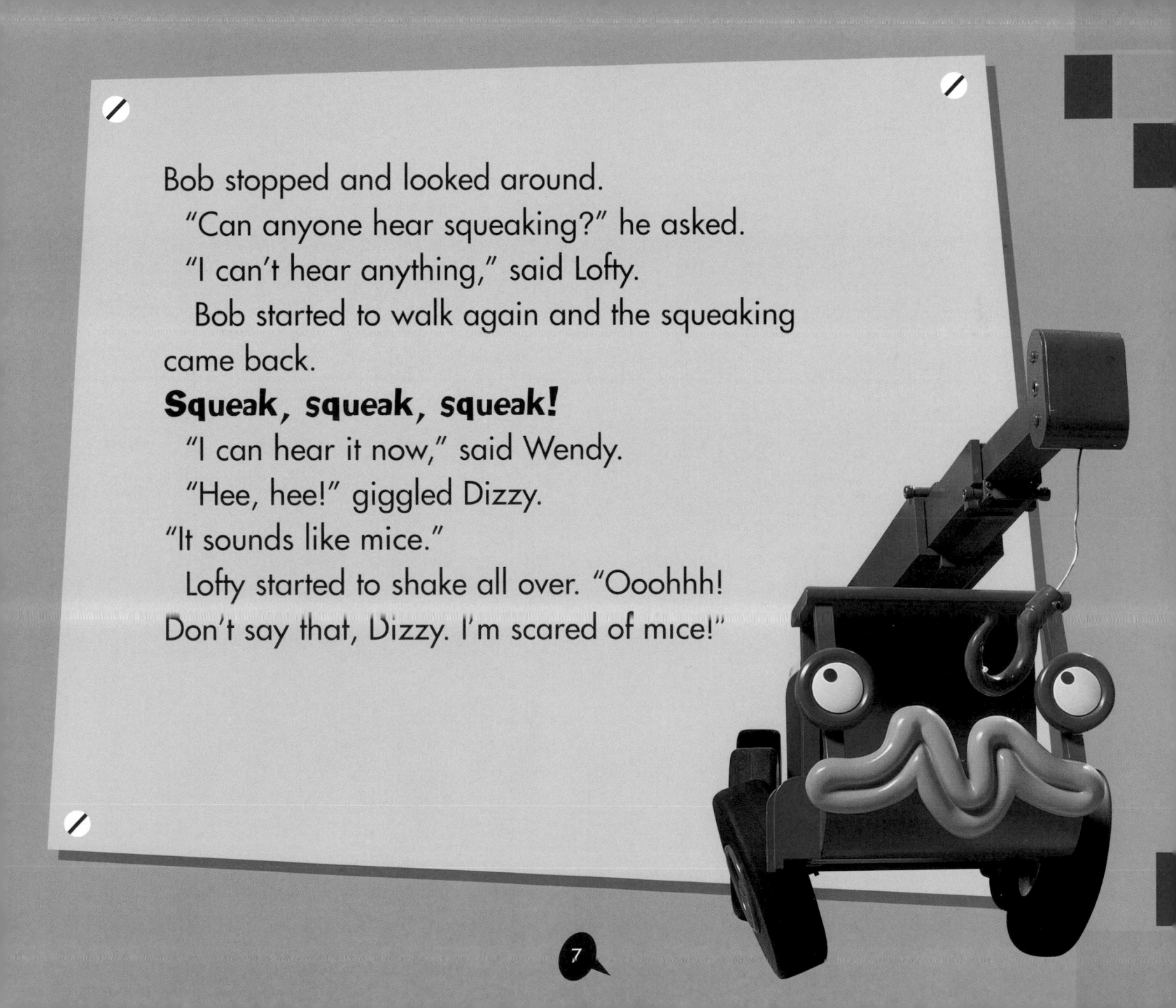

Bob stopped and looked around.

"Can anyone hear squeaking?" he asked.

"I can't hear anything," said Lofty.

Bob started to walk again and the squeaking came back.

Squeak, squeak, squeak!

"I can hear it now," said Wendy.

"Hee, hee!" giggled Dizzy. "It sounds like mice."

Lofty started to shake all over. "Ooohhh! Don't say that, Dizzy. I'm scared of mice!"

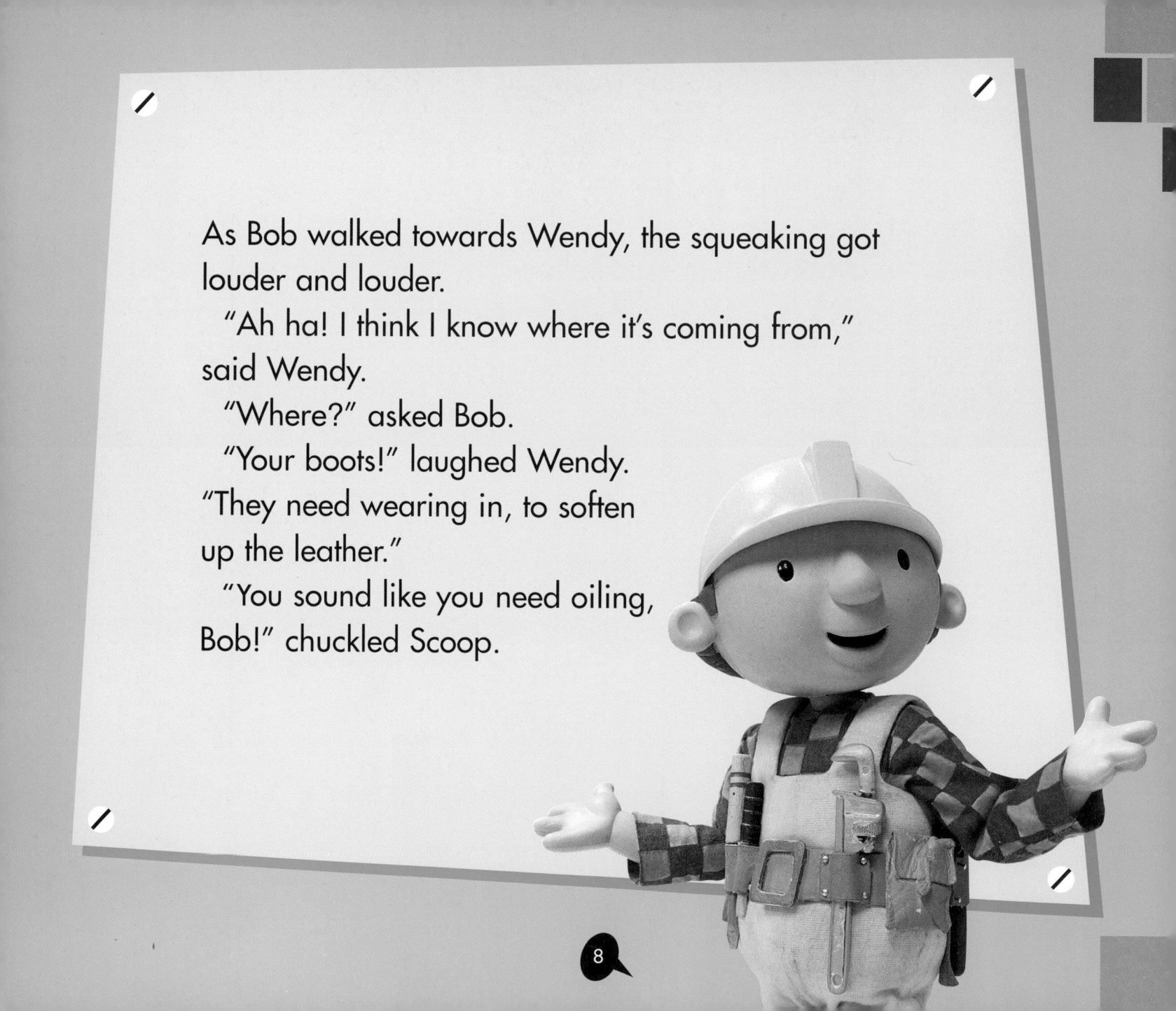

As Bob walked towards Wendy, the squeaking got louder and louder.

"Ah ha! I think I know where it's coming from," said Wendy.

"Where?" asked Bob.

"Your boots!" laughed Wendy. "They need wearing in, to soften up the leather."

"You sound like you need oiling, Bob!" chuckled Scoop.

"I think I'll walk to the job today," said Bob. "I need to wear my new boots in!"

"Come on, Lofty!" he said, and waved goodbye to the others as they set off in the opposite direction.

Lofty clattered slowly along with Bob walking behind him, carrying his lunch box.

Squeak, squeak, squeak!

Further up the lane, Bird was listening to Travis and Spud, who were trying to work out the quickest way to Bob's yard.

"You go left at the crossroads," said Spud.

"I'm sure it's right..." muttered Travis.

"No, no, no!" cried Spud.

Just then, Farmer Pickles came past, so they asked him to settle the argument.

"They say the quickest way is usually as the crow flies," he replied.

"It means the quickest way to get anywhere is to go in a straight line."

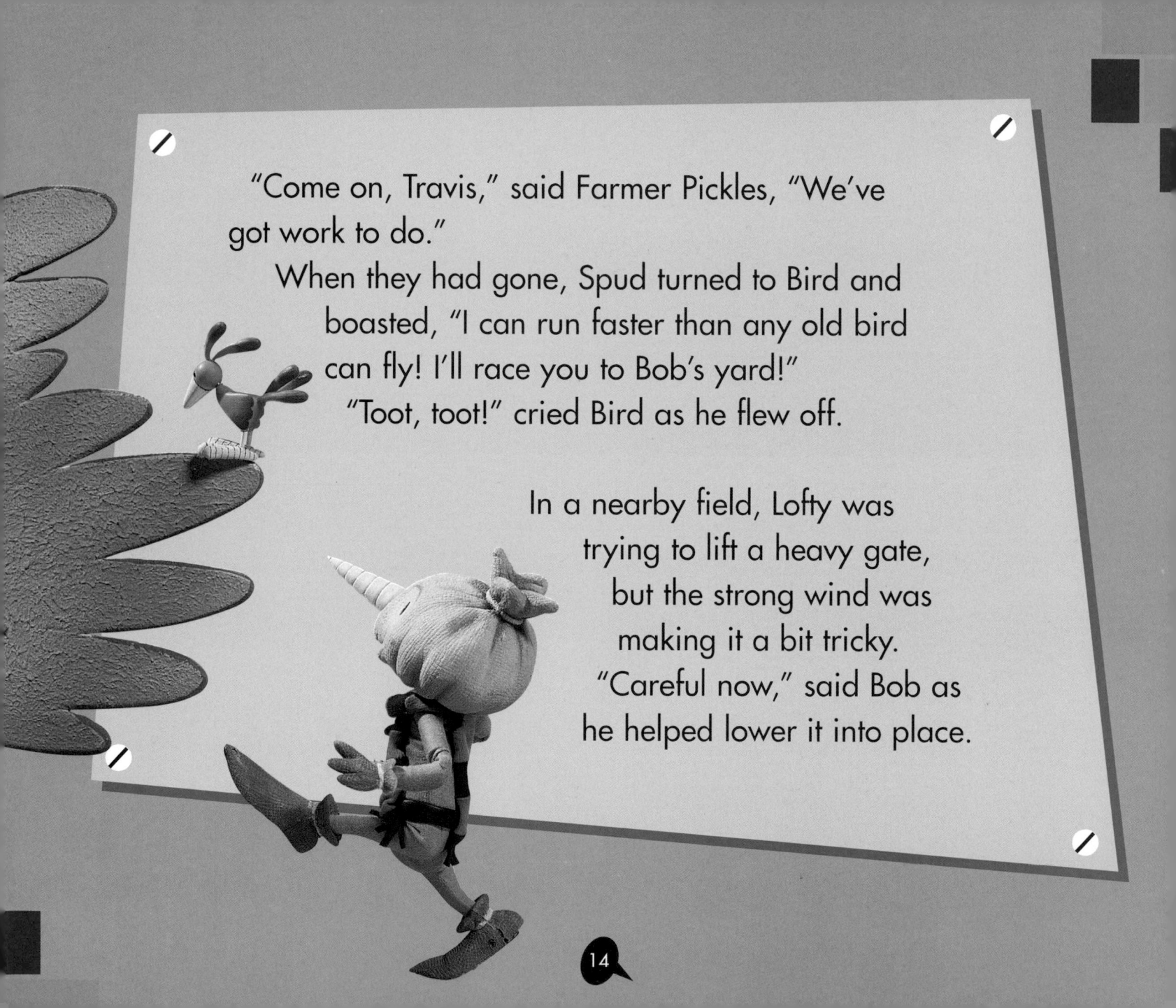

"Come on, Travis," said Farmer Pickles, "We've got work to do."

When they had gone, Spud turned to Bird and boasted, "I can run faster than any old bird can fly! I'll race you to Bob's yard!"

"Toot, toot!" cried Bird as he flew off.

In a nearby field, Lofty was trying to lift a heavy gate, but the strong wind was making it a bit tricky.

"Careful now," said Bob as he helped lower it into place.

"Phew! Time for lunch!" said Bob as he opened his lunch box.

"Oooh, what have you got today, Bob?" Lofty asked.

"My favourites! Cheese and chutney sandwiches and a big cream bun," Bob replied.

Suddenly a gust of wind blew the paper napkin from the top of Bob's sandwiches.

"Whooah!" cried Bob as he chased after it.

Meanwhile, Spud and Bird were racing across the countryside. Spud stopped when he noticed Bob's lunch box with the sandwiches and big cream bun inside.

"Mmmmm!" he said as he nibbled the sandwich. He was just about to take a big bite out of the cream bun when he spotted Bird flying away.

"I'd better save this bun until I get to Bob's yard," he said, racing off after Bird.

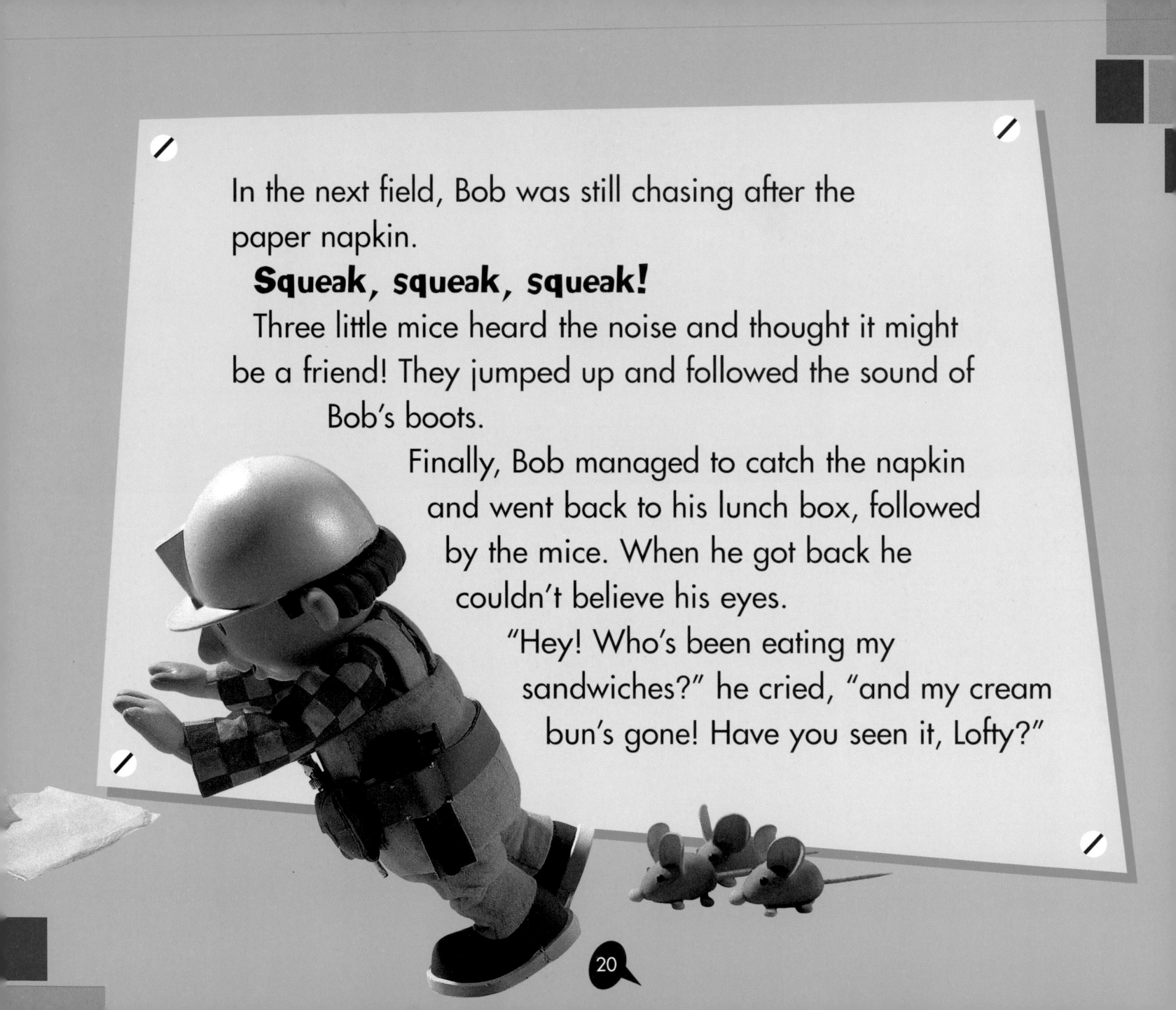

In the next field, Bob was still chasing after the paper napkin.

Squeak, squeak, squeak!

Three little mice heard the noise and thought it might be a friend! They jumped up and followed the sound of Bob's boots.

Finally, Bob managed to catch the napkin and went back to his lunch box, followed by the mice. When he got back he couldn't believe his eyes.

"Hey! Who's been eating my sandwiches?" he cried, "and my cream bun's gone! Have you seen it, Lofty?"

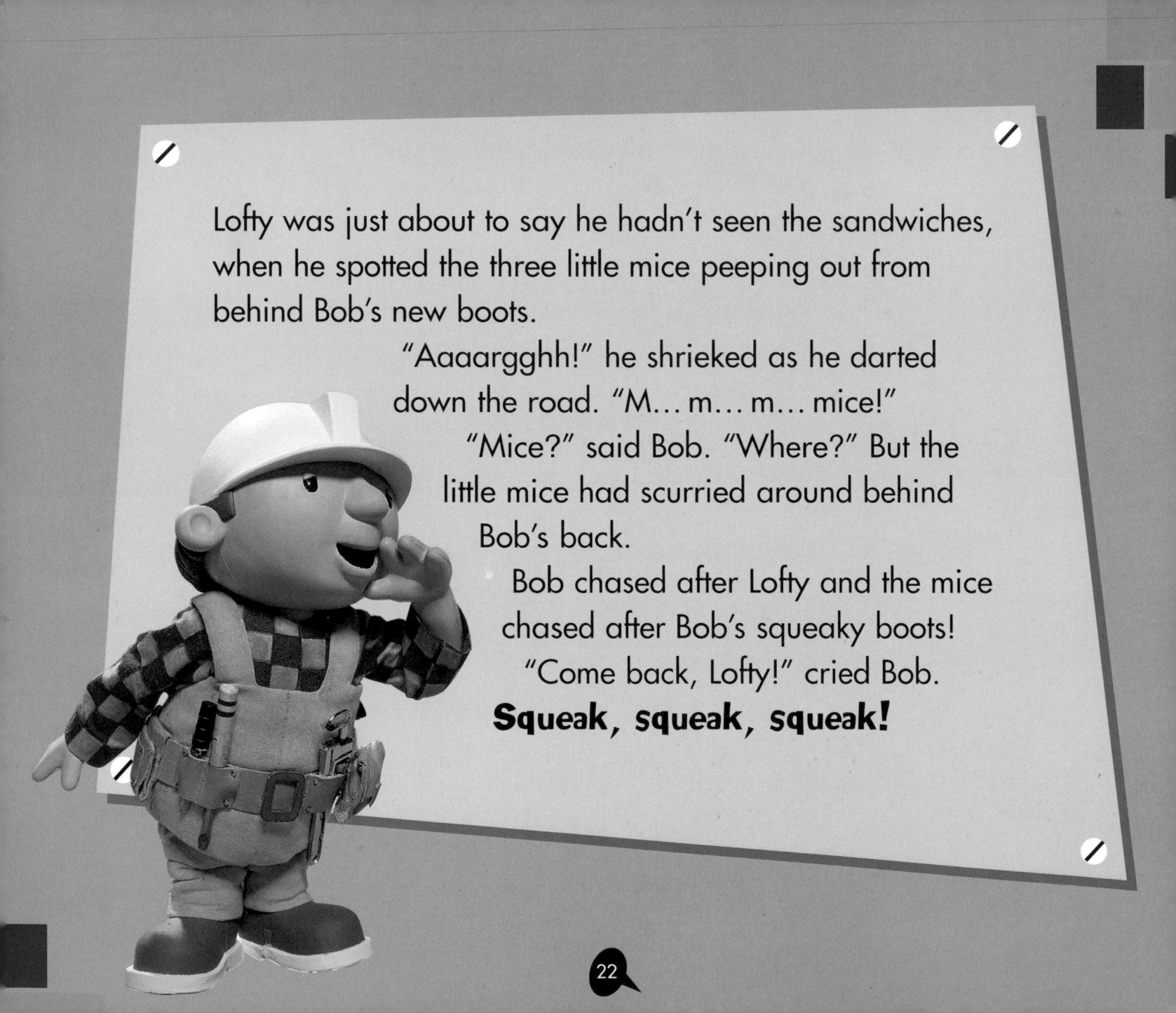

Lofty was just about to say he hadn't seen the sandwiches, when he spotted the three little mice peeping out from behind Bob's new boots.

"Aaaargghh!" he shrieked as he darted down the road. "M... m... m... mice!"

"Mice?" said Bob. "Where?" But the little mice had scurried around behind Bob's back.

Bob chased after Lofty and the mice chased after Bob's squeaky boots!

"Come back, Lofty!" cried Bob.

Squeak, squeak, squeak!

Wendy, Muck and Scoop were filling a skip with rubbish from an old kitchen, when Bird zipped overhead, followed by Spud.

"Hello, Wendy!" called Spud. "Can't stop! Bye!"

"What is going on?" puzzled Wendy.

Back at the yard Roley was snoozing and Dizzy was playing, when suddenly Lofty came roaring in.

"Umm, what's the matter, Lofty?" rumbled Roley sleepily.

"M... m... mice!" stammered Lofty. "They're chasing me!"

Bob rushed into the yard after Lofty.

"Lofty, there aren't any mice. Look!" said Bob, turning around. But this time the mice stayed still and he spotted them.

"Oooh," said Bob. "Lofty, you were right!"

The three little brown mice looked up at Bob.

Bob walked round in a circle and the mice followed him.

"Ha, ha! Look! They like my squeaky boots, don't they?"

"I don't like mice though," quivered Lofty.

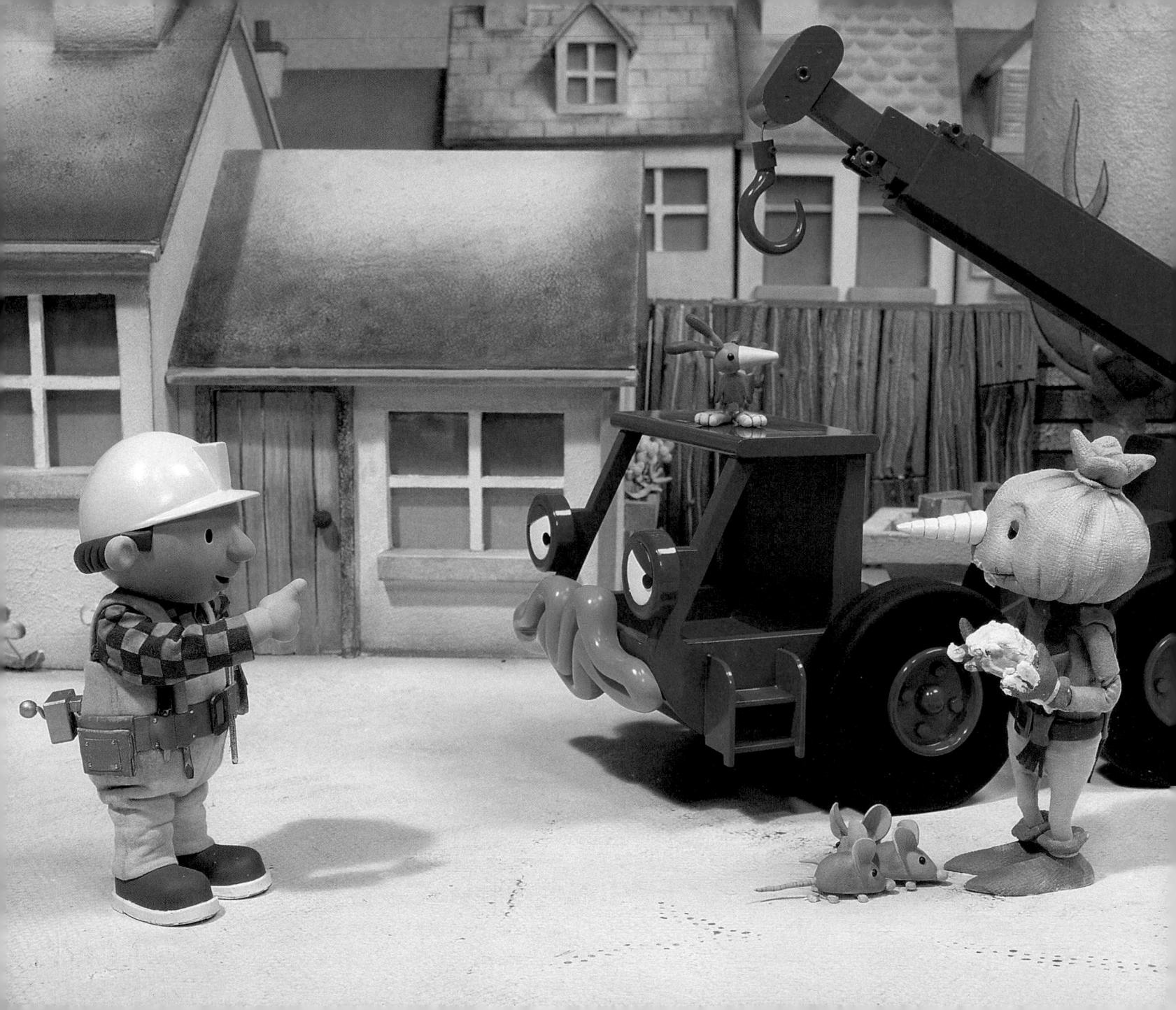

Just then, Bird came whizzing into the yard and landed on Lofty.

Spud dashed in a moment later, gasping for breath.

"I've beaten Bird!" he cried.

"Toot, toot!" whistled Bird proudly.

"Oh, no," grumbled Spud as he spotted Bird. "But at least I can eat my cream bun."

"That's my bun, isn't it?" Bob asked sternly. "You know you shouldn't take other people's things without asking."

"Sorry, Bob," mumbled Spud. Feeling embarrassed, he stared at the ground where he saw the three hungry mice looking up at him.

"Go away!" he shouted.

As Wendy, Muck and Scoop turned into the yard, they saw Spud running down the road with the three mice scampering after him.

"Leave me alone!" Spud yelled.

"**Squeak, squeak, squeak!**" went the mice as they followed him down the road.

"Hello, Wendy!" Bob called, as he walked towards her.

"Bob! Your boots have stopped squeaking," said Wendy.

"I must have worn them in with all the running about I've been doing," Bob chuckled.

"Have you had a busy day?" Wendy asked.
"Not really," Bob replied. "You could say it's been as quiet as a mouse!"

THE END!